THE
ARCTIC
FOX

For Allison
HW

For Mum
DD

LITTLE TIGER
An imprint of Little Tiger Press Limited
1 Coda Studios, 189 Munster Road,
London SW6 6AW

Imported into the EEA by Penguin Random House Ireland,
Morrison Chambers, 32 Nassau Street, Dublin D02 YH68

www.littletiger.co.uk

A paperback original
First published in Great Britain in 2024

Text copyright © Holly Webb, 2024
Illustrations copyright © David Dean, 2024
Author photograph copyright © Lou Abercrombie

ISBN: 978-1-78895-714-4

A CIP catalogue record for this book is available
from the British Library.

Printed and bound in the UK.

2 4 6 8 10 9 7 5 3 1

THE ARCTIC FOX

Holly Webb
Illustrated by David Dean

LITTLE TIGER

LONDON

"We're really going?" Ellie whispered, looking up from the shiny holiday brochure at her mum and dad.

Her mum nodded – she was smiling so hugely, it made Ellie smile too. They beamed at each other. "We're leaving the day after you break up from school," she told Ellie. "For five days, so we'll be back the day before Christmas Eve."

"I can't believe it," Ellie said, looking down at the brochure again. *Holiday Adventures in the Arctic Circle*, it said. *Visit Beautiful Lapland.*

"It looks so wild and wonderful." The picture on the front was a huge stretch of snow, so shiny and silvery-white that it mirrored the sky above, which was streaked with pink and green light. The whole place looked like something out of a fairy tale, too strange and magical to be true.

But it was real, and in three weeks' time, Ellie would be there, walking through the snow, looking up at the Northern Lights. Mum and Dad had mentioned they were going on a special surprise trip before Christmas, but she had never imagined anything as exciting as this.

"I don't even know where Lapland is," Ellie murmured.

"It's the northernmost part of Finland," Mum explained. "Further north than Norway and Sweden. The Arctic Circle is as far north as you can go!"

"It's where Santa's from," Dad pointed out, giving Ellie's little brother Taylor a squeeze. "And we're going to the village where Santa Claus lives. We get to see the man himself!"

"We're meeting Santa?" Taylor sounded confused. "At his house?"

Dad nodded. "Ellie, open the brochure and show Taylor. There's a great picture of Santa in there. And his elves!"

Ellie flicked through pages about snowmobile trips and reindeer treks, until she came to the page with Santa Claus on it, then she handed the brochure to Taylor. Her little brother sat there stroking the shiny paper, whispering to himself about elves with stripey socks, while Mum and Dad smiled at each other.

THE ARCTIC FOX

Ellie was excited about visiting the Santa Claus Village too, but it was the snow and the wild, glorious colours of the Northern Lights – the aurora – that she couldn't wait to see. Of course she'd seen snow before, but living in a city, it didn't tend to stay pretty and sparkly white for long. It quickly got churned into brown slush, and then it melted and froze and you just spent days slipping over every time you walked down the pavement. The snow in Lapland was real, deep, cold snow. It was going to be wonderful.

Santa's village had reindeer to meet too, Ellie noticed, looking over Taylor's shoulder. They looked huge in the photo, and really friendly, with children stroking them, and little silvery bells on their red harnesses. Perfect for pulling a sleigh! There would

be other animals around too, Ellie thought
– snow creatures that lived in the dark forest
surrounding the village. She'd have to find
out what they were, so she could try and spot
them. She was trying to remember the last
time they'd been to the zoo – what other
snow animals had there been, apart from
penguins and polar bears? Ellie was pretty
sure Lapland didn't have polar bears. Maybe
those fluffy white hares with the huge feet!
She'd look it up on her tablet later on.

This was the going to be the wintriest,
wildest holiday ever!

Ellie's school was getting Christmassy already.
They'd been rehearsing for the Christmas
concert for weeks now, and all the classes

were making decorations and cards to take home. But in the last week of term the festive excitement reached its peak – there seemed to be something special happening every day.

Two days before the end of term, their class was going on a trip to a museum. Ellie had been looking forward to it for ages. Their project for the autumn term had been Romans, and the museum had all sorts of Roman artefacts, as well as rooms and rooms of interesting things from all over the world. Or so their teacher Mr Jackson said. He was very, very excited about it, and he'd managed to get everyone in the class excited too. They were going there on a coach, and Ellie and her friend Leila had planned to sit together. Leila was going to have the window seat on the way there, and Ellie would have it on the way home. But all their plans had nearly been for nothing.

"You're here!" Leila yelled, flinging her arms around Ellie as she hurried, red-faced, into the playground on the morning of the trip. "Come and see Mr Jackson – he's got a list and he's ticking people off and panicking that loads of us haven't turned up yet. The coach is here, did you see?"

Ellie couldn't really have missed it – the enormous coach was parked right outside the school gates.

"Taylor was in a strop and he wouldn't put his shoes on," she told Leila, still panting a bit. "Then he didn't want to walk. Mum had to pick him up and we ran the last bit of the way. I was so scared we were going to be late!"

"You're only a bit late," Leila said soothingly. She dragged Ellie over to Mr Jackson, who ticked her off on his list, looking relieved.

"Nice to see you, Ellie, and don't worry. Your mum's already explained what happened. Now, time to get on the coach, everyone!"

The two classes started to pile on to the coach, waving excitedly to the parents who'd waited outside the gates to see them off. Ellie and Leila bagged seats together, and Ellie leaned back against hers, finally catching her breath. She'd been so relieved to see the coach still parked outside the gates.

THE ARCTIC FOX

The museum was enormous – Mr Jackson had told them it was, but that still hadn't prepared Ellie for actually being there.

The Roman gallery had statues and pots and armour, and even a huge mosaic floor that was covered in glass so you could walk on top of it and look at the patterns and pictures made from thousands of tiny tiles.

After they'd looked around and done
a worksheet, they all got to make mosaics
of their own out of little glass squares, pushed
into clay. Ellie made a big letter E, wrapped

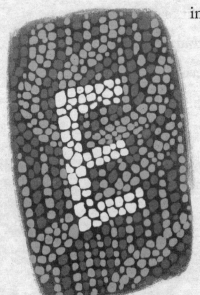

in a swirling pattern
that looked like the
Northern Lights. She
couldn't stop thinking
about them, since
she'd found out about
their trip, and she
kept trying to draw
their wonderful
sheets of colour across
the sky. It was tricky
with felt tips, though. Ellie had a feeling she
needed paint – bright, bright paint to streak
across the dark page.

They left the mosaics drying and went to eat their packed lunches. Ellie's mum had put in ginger biscuits shaped like little reindeer, enough for Leila to have some too. She said gingerbread was very traditional in Lapland, and it was called *piparkakaut* in Finnish. Mum had found a recipe and tried it out in between packing everyone's warmest clothes for the trip. Ellie's bag was sitting in the corner of her bedroom, ready to go. It gave her a little shiver of excitement every time she spotted it.

After lunch, for the last hour of the trip, they were allowed to explore some of the different galleries in the museum. Ellie and Leila studied the map, and Leila begged to go to the costume galleries. She loved clothes, and even had her own little sewing machine at home. She'd made Ellie a scrunchie for her birthday.

Luckily their teaching assistant Mrs Knowles
liked the sound of the fashion exhibits too,
and said she'd take a group to look at them.

Even though she'd really only gone to make
Leila happy, Ellie thought the clothes were
beautiful. She dawdled along in front of the
mannequins, imagining the sort of people
who'd have worn these different outfits.
So many of them were fancy, covered in

beads or jewels or embroidery, but some
of them were everyday people's clothes too.
There was a dress made out of a parachute
from the Second World War. Imagine having
no material and having to make a party frock
out of a parachute! The label said that the
parachute silk was a huge treat, and people
thought themselves lucky to have a friend
who could get them a piece.

Leila was calling. Ellie dragged herself away from the wartime dress and hurried along a line of glass cases to find her friend. She wasn't really looking at the outfits on show – but one of the figures brought her skidding to a stop. For a moment she thought the woman in the case had a cat around her neck. Ellie's aunt Rosa had a beautiful fluffy white cat called Snowdrop who lay on her shoulders like that. Auntie Rosa said he saved her pounds and pounds on her heating bills, because he was like a huge, heated scarf. He slept on top of her at night like an extra duvet too. *Was* that a cat? There hadn't been pets in any of the other displays.

It wasn't. Ellie pressed her hand against her mouth, feeling a little bit sick. It was a fox. The most beautiful, white, fluffy fox, draped around the lady's shoulders. The fox was holding one of its paws in its mouth, so the fat floofy tail draped down over the front of the lady's black velvet coat. Its eyes were made of glass, Ellie could see that they weren't real – but the fox still seemed to be staring at her.

The outfit was from around 1910, the label said. Over a hundred years old. The fox had been dead for years and years, but it still made Ellie want to cry and break the glass and pull her out. She couldn't imagine ever wanting to *wear* something like that.

Black velvet ensemble with Arctic fox stole, 1910.

Arctic foxes were trapped for their furs, and became very rare around this time due to high fur prices. However, their numbers have now recovered and they are no longer endangered.

Arctic fox. And Lapland was in the Arctic
Circle – did that mean this fox had come from
Lapland, or somewhere near there?

"Ugh. That's grim." Leila had come back to
find Ellie, and she was staring at the fox now
too. "I think it would give me nightmares, just
imagine it hanging in your wardrobe!"

Ellie shuddered, and Leila gave her a hug. "Are you OK?"

"Yeah … I just don't like it." Ellie glanced at Leila, not wanting her friend to think she was being strange. "The fox looks so sad. And – and lonely."

"I know what you mean." Leila let go and grabbed Ellie's hand instead. "Mrs Knowles sent me to find you. It's time for our turn in the shop. I bet I've got enough money to buy some chocolate, that's what you need."

In the end Leila bought chocolate and Ellie bought fudge, as well as key rings with Roman gold coins on them. They ate most of the sweets on the coach on the way home, and Leila was looking very pale and almost green by the time the coach pulled up outside the school. Ellie had managed to squash the poor white fox to the back of her mind, but she hadn't really forgotten about her. She climbed slowly down the coach steps and gave Mum a tight hug.

"What's up?" Mum hugged her back and then pulled away, looking worriedly at Ellie. "Did you get coach-sick?"

"No. I think Leila might be." Ellie slipped her hand into Mum's. Dad must be at home looking after Taylor. "I'll tell you on the way back." She waved to Leila – who still didn't look very well – and called, "See you tomorrow!"

It was hard to know how to start explaining about the fox. Ellie wasn't sure Mum was going to understand. Ellie wasn't even sure *she* understood.

Why was she so upset about something that had happened over a hundred years ago?

It had taken a while to explain about the costume galleries, and the white fox's sad glass eyes, but Mum had got it. She'd told Ellie that thankfully hardly anyone wore real fur any more.

"I think it's good that they had a fox fur in the museum, though," she said thoughtfully, as she made Ellie a mug of hot chocolate. "Sometimes I think we forget about the things humans have done to animals, for terrible reasons, and we shouldn't."

"I suppose," Ellie said doubtfully. "Where do

you think the fox came from? Could it have been from Lapland?" *Where we're going the day after the day after tomorrow!* a little voice inside her added.

"Maybe…" Mum gave her a worried look. "But Ellie, if thinking about it's going to make you upset…"

"It won't," Ellie told her, even though she wasn't quite sure. "I want to know everything about Arctic foxes. The label in the museum said they used to be really rare, because they were hunted for their fur, but they're not any more."

"OK. Let's look them up." Mum pulled out her phone. "But one thing I'm pretty sure about, Ellie, is they're super shy. I don't think we'll be spotting them on our trip, even though it would be amazing."

Ellie nodded, as if she understood, but deep down inside she was hoping that Mum was wrong. Just maybe, she'd see a beautiful white fox racing across the snow, alive and joyful.

"Oh…" Mum laughed and held out the phone to Ellie. "Look."

It was a video of a little white fox, leaping high up into the air and diving nose first into the snow. "What's it doing?" Ellie giggled.

Mum made a face. "Hunting lemmings. Apparently that's what they live on, but they're hard to catch. They have to listen for them under the snow and then dive for them. "Oh, look at it!" The fox seemed to be stuck, back legs and tail waving frantically.

It was sad about the lemmings, Ellie thought, watching as the fox finally managed to pull something that looked like a big grey mouse out of the snow. But at least the fox was going to eat it, and not just wear it to look pretty.

Mum was frowning, reading the article under the video. "Apparently Arctic foxes aren't endangered any more, but they're still very rare in Northern Europe – in countries like Finland – because they were hunted so much. This one is in the Canadian bit of the Arctic Circle."

Ellie sighed, the bubble of laughter inside her dying away. "But no one hunts them now?"

"No, they're protected," Mum said, still scanning through the article.

"OK." Ellie took a big gulp of her hot chocolate. "Can I watch the video again? Please?"

Ellie dreamed of the Arctic fox that night. Diving into the snow, snuffling and waggling her hind paws. And then falling over backwards, shaking the snow off her muzzle and thick ruff of neck fur, as if she was a bit embarrassed. She caught a lemming in the end, and then she went racing off through the tall, dark pine trees. She popped out on a great white sheet of snow, so pale and shiny that it reflected back the pink and purple glow of the Northern Lights stretching overhead.

That was the end of the dream, the white fur of the fox blurring slowly into the gleaming snow. Ellie woke up feeling happy and wishful at the same time, longing for something, though she didn't know quite what.

The last two days of term passed in a rush
– their special Christmas concert, the choir
singing carols at the retirement home,
watching a Christmas film in class. And then
it was the holidays. Ellie hugged Leila and
all her friends, and then dashed out into the
playground to find Mum and Taylor. They were
heading home to do the last bits of packing
before they set off to stay the night at a hotel
by the airport, ready to fly to Lapland the
next morning.

Ellie was ready and waiting in the hallway
half an hour after she'd got home from school.
All she'd had to do was put on her favourite
comfy clothes – jeans and her purple cardigan
with snowflakes on the pockets – which felt
perfect for travelling to a land of snow and ice.
She'd put her toy cat Emerald into her backpack

as soon as she got out of bed that morning, and she added a Christmas card that Leila had made for her at school, that said to make a snowman for her. That was all she needed to do. She sat on the bottom step of the stairs and watched Mum and Dad dashing about, putting out the rubbish and doing a last-minute water of the house plants. All the things that had to happen before a holiday. Taylor came to sit next to her on the step, and Ellie helped him put his shoes on when he held them out.

"Are we going?" he whispered.

"Soon," she whispered back.

"On a plane?"

"Yes! It's exciting! I've never been on a plane before, and neither have you. When we went on holiday to France last year, we went on the ferry, remember?"

Taylor thought for a minute. "No."

"When you had the long bread," Ellie reminded him. Taylor had fallen in love with baguettes on their camping holiday in France.

"Oh! Yes! Does Lapland have that bread?"

"I don't know…" Ellie didn't know much about the food in Lapland. Except for gingerbread. And Dad had mentioned something about fish, but Taylor wasn't going to want to eat that unless it was fish fingers.

But there was bound to be something similar, wasn't there? "Probably," she added hurriedly, since Taylor was looking worried.

"OK! Time to go!" Dad came down the stairs carrying two large bags, and Ellie jumped up so he could get past her.

"Now? We're really going now?" she asked hopefully.

Dad beamed at her, and Ellie realized that he was just as excited as she was. "This very minute."

Ellie pushed the two halves of the seat belt together and leaned over to look out of the window. There were planes everywhere, and strange trucks bustling around, pulling carts that Mum had said were people's luggage, or meals for passengers. She'd never seen anything like it before. So many people, all rushing around, and planes taking off every minute, lifting up into the air and roaring past the windows of the departure lounge. Ellie couldn't help holding her breath every time she saw it happening – how could something so huge just rise up into the sky?

Mum had explained to Ellie that they were only going on a plane because this was a special holiday. They wouldn't be flying very often, probably not for another few years now, because flights were bad for the environment. But it would take a long time to get to Lapland any other way.

Ellie had expected the plane to feel stranger – but apart from the tiny windows, it wasn't that different to the coach they'd been on to go to the museum. She looked in the pocket on the back of the seat in front of her, and found a sick bag. Ellie hoped she wouldn't need it. She'd eaten all that chocolate and fudge on the coach and not felt sick like Leila. Perhaps she wouldn't be airsick either. There was a magazine in the pocket too, all about the different places the airline flew to – mostly the countries in Scandinavia.

"Ellie, you need to watch this," Mum said, tapping her arm gently and pointing up at the screen above their heads. It was starting to play a safety film, all about what to do if there was a problem with the plane.

"Don't worry," Mum whispered. "They have to tell us this so we know what to do just in case, but planes are really safe."

The magazine was still on Ellie's lap as they

took off – she held tightly to Mum's hand, gasping together at that weird moment when they felt the plane lift off the ground. Ellie stared out of the window as the airport and the houses and roads all around it dwindled away into tiny toys, and then the plane settled above the clouds, and there wasn't much more to see. Ellie flicked through the magazine, wondering if there would be anything about Santa's village, Rovaniemi.

But as she turned the pages, Ellie suddenly stopped, her breath caught in her throat. Looking out from the magazine was a beautiful, fluff-furred white fox with a pointed nose and shining black eyes.

Ellie gazed at the photo for a moment, spellbound as the creature from her dreams stared back at her. Then, slowly, she started to read the article. It was about the national parks in Finland, which were trying to increase the numbers of Arctic foxes. It explained that Arctic foxes lived on the tundra, which was the high land above the treeline. Ellie puzzled over this for a moment and then decided it must mean the bits where the ground was too high up for trees to grow.

THE ARCTIC FOX

It said Arctic foxes weren't always white, either. Their fur would change to black or grey in the summer time, so they were camouflaged. That made sense, Ellie thought. It was no good being a bright white fox against green grass and plants. The white camouflage would only work in perfect snow. And that was getting rarer due to climate change, since lots of countries weren't getting as much snow as they once did. The white foxes were losing the special advantage they'd had over red foxes. Now the red foxes could spread further into white fox territory, and the two were competing for the same food – but the red foxes were bigger, and fiercer, and stronger...

At the moment, the article said, there were only about four hundred and fifty Arctic foxes in all of Norway, Sweden and Finland. Ellie chewed worriedly on her bottom lip.

Mum had said Arctic foxes were rare, but there were four hundred and fifty people at her school, and her school wasn't very big. Only that many foxes in three whole countries?

The article went on to say that most years they only saw between ten and twenty Arctic foxes in all of Finland. And Finland was huge! Nearly one and a half times the size of Britain. This was *good* news, though, it said. This was after the national parks' team had given the white foxes extra food and tried to protect them from the red foxes. Before that, there had only been about a hundred foxes.

Now an Arctic fox pair had even had pups in Lapland – that hadn't happened for years and years. It was a huge success story – just those three little pups.

Ellie hadn't realized just how rare "rare" meant.

Ellie twitched in her sleep, leaping with the white fox, diving deep into the snow. She could hear squeaks and skittering paws below the hard crust, and she was hungry. She buried her nose in the thick snow, plunging down into the lemmings' tunnel – but the creatures had already fled. She pulled back out, shaking her muzzle and ears crossly.

She would try again, further down towards the trees. The white fox pattered across the surface, ears pricked and listening. There were more lemmings about – she could hear the faintest squeaking, a feathery rustle under the snow. She tracked this way and that, her ears swivelling. She was so focused on the sounds that she didn't see the snare until she'd run straight into it. The loop of wire caught around her neck, and she shrieked in fright and anger, trying desperately to pull back out of the trap. But she was caught fast, the wire already cutting deep through her fur…

She woke in a panic, breathing in short gasps and pulling at her neck.

"Ellie, are you OK? Are you feeling sick? I thought you were asleep." Mum was leaning over her worriedly. "I was about to wake you up to show you the snow – we're nearly landing!"

Ellie blinked at her mum, and then looked around the plane, the snow-covered tundra fading as she watched passengers putting their seat belts on, ready for landing. She was in a plane. Already she couldn't remember what had frightened her so much. Something bad had happened, she'd been trapped, but she wasn't sure how…

It had been a dream; that was all. That was what Ellie tried to tell herself, anyway. Even though she couldn't remember exactly what had happened, she knew she'd never had a dream that felt so real.

"Aren't they the biggest snowmen you've ever seen?" Dad said, laughing. He lifted Taylor up to sit on his shoulders, but the snowman was still taller than both of them. Ellie bounced lightly in her snow boots – she still hadn't got used to the way the snow squeaked when you walked on it.

THE ARCTIC FOX

"I don't think I've seen Christmas
trees that tall either," Mum murmured,
squeezing Ellie's hand in her mitten.

The whole of Rovaniemi seemed to be
full of tall fir trees, as though the town
was a clearing in a huge forest.

Here in Santa's village, the trees were swathed in golden fairy lights, as well as great clumps of snow all along the branches. They looked magical, dotted about between the log cabins with their white roofs.

THE ARCTIC FOX

They'd gone for a little walk the afternoon before, when they'd arrived – just to get their bearings, Dad said, and to find somewhere to have dinner. It felt very odd, the way the town was just used to such a harsh winter. Back home this much snow would be exciting. Ellie's school would be having a snow day, and everyone would be out building snowmen or sledging. Here, people just got on with life. Everything was made for the cold, it seemed. Ellie had spotted someone on a scooter, but instead of wheels, there were skis. The man scooted along, pushing with one foot, just like Ellie did with her scooter at home. She was longing to try one.

The light was different here too. Ellie knew that it was mid-morning – they'd caught the bus to Santa's village just after breakfast –

but if felt like a late winter afternoon.

Dad had explained that it was because they were so far north – Rovaniemi was on the border of the Arctic Circle – in Santa's village there were tall pillars all along the line that showed where the Arctic Circle started. This meant that in the middle of summer the sun never set and there was no night, and now in December the sun never properly rose. Ellie wasn't sure she'd want to spend the whole winter here. The sky was lit by a strange twilight, and the light seemed to reflect back from the snow. It felt almost ghostly – when they weren't surrounded by fairy lights and Christmas trees.

"Can we see Santa now?" Taylor pleaded, and Dad carefully lowered him back down.

"Don't worry, he knows we're coming.

We're just going to look around the village for a bit first. Maybe meet the reindeer!"

There was a little paddock close to Santa's big log cabin, where the reindeer were waiting to be admired and patted. They were so much bigger than Ellie had thought they would be, with enormous, spreading antlers. Their red harnesses were scattered with tiny silver bells, which jingled whenever they moved. Ellie took her gloves off to touch their velvety noses, even though the big thermometer on the way in had said it was minus eleven degrees. The reindeer felt warm, even if the air didn't. But she only lasted a few seconds without her gloves – it was freezing!

Ellie loved standing there in the snow though, watching the great creatures snort and stamp their hooves.

The paddock was surrounded by more of the huge, dark fir trees, and she kept thinking that any moment a little white fox face would peer round one of the trunks. She knew it wouldn't happen really – Arctic foxes were found higher up, out on the wild tundra, they wouldn't come here, where there were lights and music and chatter and excitement. But still, Ellie couldn't stop watching, looking at the glimmering paths between the trees, and hoping that a faint shadow was really a puff of white fur.

"Shall we go and see Santa then?" Mum asked at last, and they headed back to the log cabin, past an enormous clock that stretched between the floors.

It had a huge, swinging pendulum that was bigger than Taylor, and shiny golden letters on the front that said it was only five days until Christmas.

Ellie felt her heart thudding with excitement as they reached the top of the steps and the door to Santa's room. She could hear a deep rolling laugh as he talked to the family in front of them in the line. The children's voices were squeaky with delight. Taylor was hopping up and down next to her, hanging on to Dad's hand.

It seemed ages until it was their turn to meet Santa and have their photo taken, but at last an elf in a pointy red hat and stripey leggings under his shorts ushered them in, leading them up to Santa Claus, who was sitting on a huge wooden chair. There were benches next to him for them to sit down too.

Ellie looked shyly up at Santa Claus – *Joulupukki*, he was called here in Finland – and saw his eyes sparkling at her, almost buried under a red hat and an explosion of curly white beard.

"I'll be seeing you again soon," Santa was telling Taylor seriously. "Have you been good? What about your sister? Has she been nice?"

Taylor was too shy to say anything. He just nodded as hard as he could and made a sort of small *eep* noise.

"That's very good to hear. Make sure you're
fast asleep on Christmas Eve, won't you?"

They headed back out into the snow again,
past the post office, shelves piled high with
letters to Santa. Taylor was clutching tightly
at the envelope with their photograph in.

The next morning, Ellie's family were setting off on the second part of their trip, a long drive further north to the village of Inari. It was a special place, Dad explained to Ellie and Taylor. It was a village where the Sámi people in Finland had their parliament, and a museum, and where they held lots of festivals and celebrations of their culture. Their homeland was called Sápmi, and it spread across part of Norway, Sweden and Finland. Lots of the Sámi people had been travelling reindeer herders, living in tents as they followed their reindeer to different grazing grounds. The Inari Sámi were different, though – they'd mostly lived by fishing in the huge lake close to the village, and by hunting wild reindeer.

Ellie and her family were going to stay

in a log cabin just outside the village, among the pine trees. Mum said it would be like getting back to nature – they'd be able to go exploring in the forest and out to the tundra, the land higher up above the village. Maybe even a special trip on snowshoes across the frozen lake. It was a chance to spot incredible wildlife too – there were even wild wolves and lynx in parts of Finland. Ellie had given Mum a shocked look, but Mum explained that wolves weren't really dangerous to people – they wanted to keep out of humans' way as much as they could, and the same for lynx. Ellie hadn't even known what lynx were – a sort of wild cat with a very short tail and tufty ears, apparently.

The most exciting thing was they might get to see the Northern Lights. Inari was much further north than Rovaniemi, and it was supposed to be a really good place to view the aurora.

It was nearly four hours of driving to get to Inari, though. The snowy countryside was beautiful and strange at first, but after a while, it all started to look the same. Even the frozen lakes that Mum kept pointing out didn't feel exciting. Ellie settled into a daydream, thinking about the wonderful photos she'd seen in the holiday brochure. She'd almost forgotten about the Northern Lights in the excitement of seeing Santa Claus, but now she was imagining those sheets of purple and green light streaming across the sky again. She remembered racing across the snow with her brothers and sisters, with the lights blazing overhead...

Ellie blinked, shaking away those strange half memories. Of course she'd never seen the Northern Lights, neither had Mum and Dad, that was why it was so special. And she didn't have any sisters! She must have been half asleep, lulled by the movement of the car.

They were going out to look for the Northern Lights that night – Mum had booked a guide to take them to the best place. She'd warned Ellie and Taylor that the aurora didn't come every night, though. They had to be lucky and hope for the right weather.

Ellie crossed her fingers as tightly as she could.

"Ellie… Ellie, wake up, love. We're here." Dad was unclipping Ellie's seat belt and gently shaking her. She blinked out at the little cabin, snuggled in the snow under the tall pines. It looked like something out of a fairy tale.

The owners of the cabin had given them
a code to get the key out of a box by the door,
so they could get straight in, just as if the
cabin was their own little house. Ellie and
Taylor went round exploring and admiring
everything – the windows looking out at the

forest, the little bedroom up a ladder on a sort of balcony in the roof, the black iron wood-burning stove with a basket of firewood all ready beside it. Dad said they might even be able to toast marshmallows.

Mum and Dad were going to sleep upstairs – they were a bit worried about Ellie and especially Taylor having to come down the ladder in the middle of the night, in case they needed the loo. Ellie and Taylor were sharing the downstairs bedroom, where there were two single beds, covered in red and white quilts.

"Oh, they've left us some supplies, look," Mum said, reading a little card sticking out of a basket on the kitchen counter. "Biscuits, and they say there's some milk in the fridge. And here's some directions to the shops. Perfect. We should go and get something for

dinner before we get too settled in and
we don't want to move…"

"Pizza!" Taylor skidded into the kitchen.
"I want pizza!"

"I don't know … pizza's not very Finnish,"
Dad started to say, and Ellie looked at Taylor
worriedly. There weren't many foods Taylor
liked, and it worried him when he had to eat
something strange. Pizza was easy and he knew
he liked it. Some of the food they'd had so far
had been a bit spicy and different, and he'd
mostly eaten bread – telling him there was
no pizza now wasn't going to go down well.

"I'm sure there'll be pizza," Mum said
soothingly. "We'll see what we can find.
Do you want to come, Taylor? You can help
me choose?"

But Taylor was tired and grumpy and

he'd been in a car for four hours and he just wanted someone to find him a pizza right now. "I want pizza!" he wailed. "I hate it! I hate it! I want pizza!"

Ellie decided the best thing to do was get out of the way. She slipped quietly from the kitchen, and left Mum and Dad to calm her little brother down. She went into the bedroom and curled up on the cushioned window seat, looking out at the trees. She could still hear Taylor crying next door, but it sounded as though he was quietening down a bit.

Maybe they could go out and build a snowman later, to help cheer Taylor up? Or a snow pizza, Ellie thought, smiling to herself. He'd like that. She was just thinking about how to make a snow sculpture actually look like a pizza, when a tiny dark creature sped out on to the snow, stopping to dig furiously with its front paws.

Ellie pressed her nose against the window, staring. It was hard to see in the winter light, but she supposed it was a squirrel – not a chunky grey squirrel like the ones she knew from home, though. This was definitely smaller. Now that the squirrel was darting closer into the light from the cabin, Ellie could see that it had tall, tufted red ears – and red paws too, even if most of its fur was greyish. She watched it skittering about, digging every so often at the base of a tree trunk, and wondered if it was looking for its food stores. Had it lost them?

She was so busy watching the red squirrel, giggling at the grumpy way it kept stopping to dig, that she almost missed the fox.

The squirrel didn't.
It shot up the nearest pine
tree faster than Ellie would
have believed possible. The
white fox slunk out from behind
the next tree, and stood up on
her hind paws, front paws on the
tree trunk, looking regretfully up
into the branches. Ellie guessed
that the squirrel was squeaking
rudely at it from somewhere
high up above.

The fox sat back down in the snow, looking annoyed with herself – and then she glanced up. Perhaps she could feel Ellie watching her.

"You're not meant to be here," Ellie whispered against the glass. "You're not a forest creature, your white fur's going to show up against the trees. What are you doing down here?"

Perhaps the fox was hungry, and exploring through the woods for food, she wondered. The article in the magazine had said that some years Arctic foxes struggled if there weren't many lemmings around. That was why the national parks' team had been putting out extra food for them.

Ellie's breath was misting the window glass, and she wiped it away hurriedly with her sleeve. When the glass was clear again, the little white fox was gone.

If she had ever been there at all.

Later that evening, a smiley Finnish girl called Anneli came to pick them up for the Northern Lights trip. Ellie liked her – she had bright blue eyes and a rainbow knitted scarf tucked into her layers of coats. Anneli even managed to cheer up Taylor, who'd woken from an afternoon nap feeling grumpy. He wasn't keen on the idea of walking around in the snow looking up at the sky.

"Let's get you all in the car," Anneli explained, "and we'll go and meet…" Then she trailed off, suddenly looking a bit worried.

Ellie noticed that Mum and Dad were making faces at her.

So there was a secret – something she and Taylor weren't supposed to know. Ellie thought about telling them she'd seen, but then decided not to. The trip had been wonderful so far, even with her strange dreams about the fox and the Northern Lights. She didn't mind there being a secret – it just made everything feel more Christmassy and special.

Ellie was sleepy too, but heading out into the polar night was exciting, even if it was just another car journey to start with. It felt like an adventure. Taylor was falling asleep again though, snuggled up against Mum in the back seat – Ellie hoped he didn't sleep through whatever the surprise was.

"Here we are," Anneli announced at last,

stopping the car. "Are you ready for this? I've got a good feeling about tonight, the sky's so clear." She turned to smile over the back of her seat at Ellie and a yawning Taylor. "Come and meet my friends."

"What are we doing?" Ellie whispered to Dad as he helped her out of the car on to the ice. "What does she mean, her friends?"

Dad was grinning, like he was desperate to tell but still holding himself back. "Just wait and see. Only a couple of minutes, Ellie, I promise. You'll love it."

Anneli led them through the snow to a timber building where shadowy figures were waiting, half lit by lamps. As they came closer, Ellie realized that the shadows were reindeer, harnessed to three beautiful scarlet wooden sleighs.

"Do we get to go in those?" Ellie whispered, her eyes widening.

"Yes!" Mum smiled. "I thought you'd like it. I was so pleased when you loved the reindeer at Santa's village. And don't worry, Ellie," she added. "We're still going to look for the Northern Lights – it's just we're going by reindeer!"

"And we get dinner," Dad added. "Sausages cooked on a big campfire, while we're watching for the aurora."

"Sausages!" Taylor still sounded sleepy, but sausages had definitely cheered him up.

Anneli introduced them to the reindeer, Kalevi, Ansa and Meri, and then helped them into the sleighs. She was going to drive the front one, pulled by Meri, and the other two reindeer were trained to follow her out to the place where they would wait for the aurora. Ellie snuggled up next to Dad and helped him hold the reins. It was exciting to feel Kalevi pulling, even if they weren't really telling him what to do.

They sped through the dark night, the sleigh runners hissing against the snow. Ellie kept peering up at the sky, hoping to see those bright streaks of light.

"Does it look a bit green over there?" she asked
Dad hopefully.

Dad screwed up his eyes. "Maybe? It's hard to
tell, isn't it? I think once we see it, we'll know."

At last they pulled up outside another wooden hut, this one with a tall pointed roof, and an open space at the front where they could sit and watch the sky. There were comfy-looking camp chairs along the open bit, with warm blankets draped over them. Anneli led the reindeer round the side of the hut to take them out of their sleigh harness, and then bustled back with a big jug of hot juice – Ellie wasn't quite sure what kind of fruit was in it, but it tasted like delicious spicy blackcurrant.

She was just holding out her cup to Anneli for a refill, when Mum suddenly gasped.

"Look! Look!"

"Lights!" Taylor squeaked.

Anneli put down the jug and crouched beside Ellie, pointing up at the sky. "There! You see? The fox is running!"

Ellie hardly heard her – she was staring upwards, her mouth open, almost forgetting to breathe. It wasn't the same as in photographs. Ellie hadn't understood what it would be like to have the lights falling down around you. It reminded her of the fireworks display they'd been to, back in November, where the rockets seemed to burst into waterfalls of shimmering lights. Great masses of eerie green were tumbling towards them now, slowly swirling across the sky. It felt as if soon the lights would come close enough to touch.

"That's amazing…" Dad whispered, and he reached out his hand to hold tight on to Ellie's. "Isn't it magical?"

The colours were changing now – the bright green was fading into a softer violet blue, and then a glowing edge of pink all along the top.

They watched for about twenty minutes, and then the colours gradually ebbed away, leaving the sky velvet dark and sprinkled with stars.

"You were lucky," Anneli told them. "That was one of the best I've seen in a long time. And good timing too – Mikael will have your dinner ready in a minute."

It was as they were eating by the fire that Ellie remembered what Anneli had said when the lights first appeared. "What did you mean before, when you said the fox was running?"

Anneli smiled at her. "It's an old story. In Finland we call the aurora the foxfire – *revontulet*. The little fox runs across the snow, and she sweeps the snow crystals up into the air. She brushes her tail against the tree branches and sparks fly up, and it all makes the most magical fires across the sky."

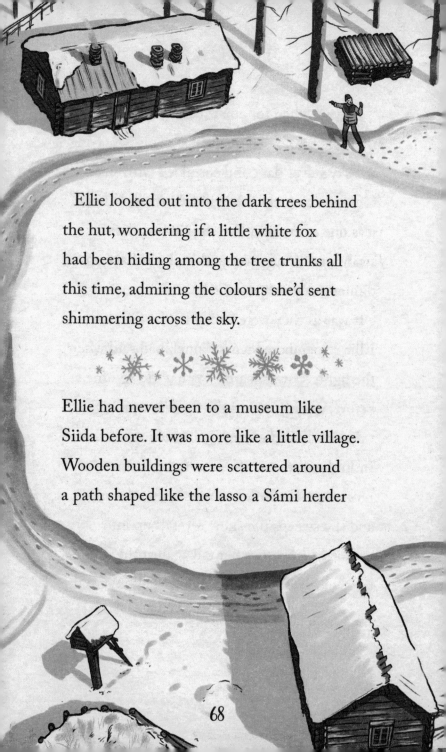

Ellie looked out into the dark trees behind
the hut, wondering if a little white fox
had been hiding among the tree trunks all
this time, admiring the colours she'd sent
shimmering across the sky.

Ellie had never been to a museum like
Siida before. It was more like a little village.
Wooden buildings were scattered around
a path shaped like the lasso a Sámi herder

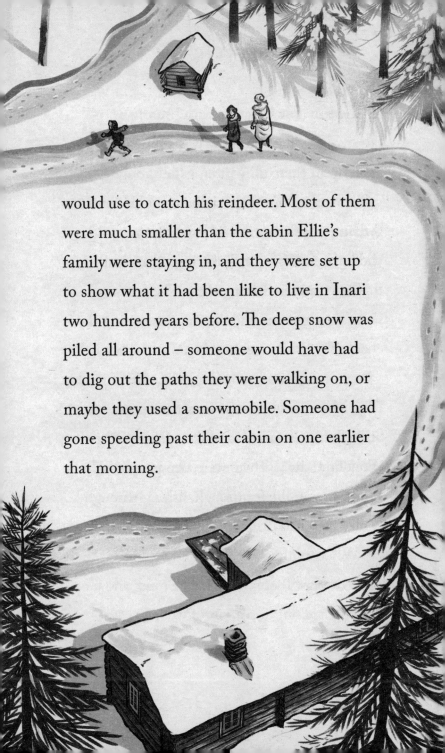

would use to catch his reindeer. Most of them were much smaller than the cabin Ellie's family were staying in, and they were set up to show what it had been like to live in Inari two hundred years before. The deep snow was piled all around – someone would have had to dig out the paths they were walking on, or maybe they used a snowmobile. Someone had gone speeding past their cabin on one earlier that morning.

The tiny houses must have been hard to live in when the snow was shutting you up in them all winter, Ellie thought, shivering a little. Especially in midwinter, when it was so dark and everything would be lit by firelight or flickering oil lamps.

They wandered along the paths, peering into the different buildings and admiring the beautiful old sledges and boats in the big hall. The museum was built along the side of Lake Inari, but the water was frozen solid now – Ellie hadn't even realized it *was* water when they first saw it. There were two people right out there on the ice though, fishing through holes they had drilled.

"What are those?" Ellie asked, looking at the next display. There were strange ropes and loops of wire laid out, and a sort of wooden cage.

"They're for catching reindeer, I think."
Mum was reading the signs. "It's a lasso –
and some other ways of trapping animals…"
She glanced down at Ellie a little anxiously.
"It's how the people here survived, Ellie, by
trapping their food. And they made a lot of
their clothes from fur because they needed
it to keep warm."

"I know," Ellie said, her voice very small.
"But the animals needed it more. Did they
catch Arctic foxes with traps like that?"

"With snares, I think," Mum said sadly.
"Let's go on."

"You know it's illegal to trap Arctic foxes
here these days," Dad said, as they hurried
on to look at a Sámi tent. "It would never
happen now."

"I know," Ellie muttered. It wasn't making

her feel a lot better, though. Not everyone who wore fox fur had wanted it to keep warm in the winter snow. The scarf in the museum back home had been made to look fashionable, not to keep out the cold.

"I'm getting chilly," Mum murmured. "Shall we hurry along this last bit and go into the indoor museum?"

Ellie trudged after her through the snow, trying to forget about the horrible snares. She kept worrying about that white fox she'd seen from the cabin. Ellie still wasn't sure if the fox had actually been there, or if she'd just imagined her. But would she have dreamed up a fox chasing a squirrel? How would she even have known about red squirrels?

There are no more snares, Ellie told herself, as she wandered around the museum's glass cases. *She's safe.* She couldn't help thinking about that fox's great-great-grandparents who hadn't been, though… She tried to focus on Anneli's story about the foxfire instead, the little fox sweeping snow up into the sky. Foxes' tails were even called brushes, weren't they? It all fitted together. *I wonder if they call a fox's tail a brush in Finnish too,* Ellie wondered.

"Ellie, come and see this!" Mum was calling, and Ellie went to find her. She was looking into one of the cases, full of what seemed to be rather boring pieces of dark grey stone. Ellie couldn't imagine why she sounded so excited. Then the light changed a little, or perhaps Ellie turned her head, and the stones blazed with colour.

"What…?" Ellie gasped, watching the stones glimmer pink and purple and green.

THE ARCTIC FOX

"It's spectrolite," Mum said. "Apparently it's a stone that you can only find in Finland."

"It's like the Northern Lights," Ellie whispered. "The way the colours move."

"People here say it's like the Northern Lights come down to earth," Mum told her, smiling.

Ellie touched her fingertips to the glass, wishing she could hold one of the stones. It would be like having the eerie, wonderful aurora in her hand.

Essi snuffled into her bedclothes, made a little
snorting noise, and then woke up, blinking
and yawning in the sudden light. It was
seeping into the cabin through the cracks in
the wooden shutters, an eerie greenish glow
lighting up the floorboards. Essi pulled the
blanket around her, shivering. The cabin was
so cold. She could feel the icy wind coming
through the walls.

She was wide awake now. Essi glanced
enviously over at her little brother, curled up
and snoozing on the other side of the room,

close to the banked-down fire. He looked so comfortable. She could hear her parents' soft breathing too. Everyone was fast asleep, except for her. She should probably wrap herself up tightly in her blanket and try to get back to sleep – but the foxfire was glimmering across the cabin, and dancing inside her. She didn't want to be indoors.

Moving as quietly as she could, Essi unwound herself from the blanket, and crept over to the wooden storage box in the corner to find her clothes. She pulled on thick leggings and a warm embroidered wool dress, and then padded across to the door to find her outdoor coat and boots. The foxfire was bright enough to see by – almost, anyway. She stumbled over her little brother by the fire, making him wriggle and moan, but he didn't wake up. And more importantly, neither did her parents.

She felt for her outdoor things, wrapping herself up as warmly as she could, and pulling her hat down tight over her ears. Then she undid the latch and slipped out into the snow.

The foxfire was hanging there in the sky up above her, yellow green just shading into blue as far up as she could see.

THE ARCTIC FOX

Essi stretched her arms out wide and turned her face up to the light. She could feel it surrounding her, filling her with a wild winter magic. After days and days of blue half darkness, the foxlight was making her feel giddy. She wanted to dance. Essi glanced cautiously back towards the cabin. She was almost silent in the snow, but it would be safer to get further away, in case her parents woke up – they'd be furious with her for going outside on her own in the middle of the night. She hurried away through the belt of trees that surrounded the cabin, up to the higher ground beyond. It was a steep climb, and she was puffing for breath by the time she came out on to open snow.

The foxfire was even grander out here. Airy blue-green curtains dropped down from the sky, reflecting back from the frozen snow. It was like a strange land – Essi almost expected to see trolls or *tontut* sprites dancing among the lights. She stepped out on to the fields and spun slowly round, feeling the foxfire shimmering inside her.

She was still spinning when she heard a faint, eerie wail across the snow. She stopped, her heart suddenly thumping. What was that?

Was it her little brother? He hadn't followed her, had he? The cry came again and Essi shook her head. She didn't think it was a child. It was a sharper, stranger sound. She looked up again at the lights in the sky – she'd never heard a sound from them before, but she had been thinking they were full of fairies… No, it was a *real* noise. Eerie but … frightened? Or hurt, maybe. What should she do?

Her first thought was to go and help. Whoever or whatever was making that noise sounded desperate. Essi looked uncertainly back towards the woods and her cabin.

She knew exactly what her father would say. It wasn't safe to be outside on her own, and she was taking dangerous risks, especially at night. She couldn't disappear off even further away from home, towards who-knew-what.

Essi sighed, and did it anyway.

The mournful cries were still echoing across the snow. Was she imagining it, or were they sounding weaker now? She trudged a little faster, wishing she'd thought to bring her snowshoes. Her boots were sinking into the ground whenever she broke through the frozen crust, and she hadn't tied the straps round them tightly enough in her hurry to leave the house. Snow was getting in around the top. If she wasn't careful, her mother would notice that she'd been outside.

Her boots… Essi stared down at them. Reindeer-hide *nuvttot* that her mother had sewn for her, fastened with embroidered straps that she'd stitched herself over the summer.

Why did they suddenly look so strange?

They'd bought her new boots for their holiday.

Mum had said she'd need proper waterproof snow boots, that it was important to keep their feet warm and dry in such a cold place.

Ellie stopped there in the snow, her breath catching. What was she *doing*, out on her own? She shouldn't be out here! If Mum and Dad woke up, or Taylor, they'd be panicking.

She spun around, trying to spot the path she'd followed through the trees. Had she been sleepwalking? She couldn't remember why she'd got out of bed. It was so cold. She tucked her mittened hands under her armpits, shivering.

It wasn't just the boots. All of her clothes were different. Boots and coat and mittens all seemed to be made out of some sort of fur – maybe reindeer hide. Like the traditional Sámi clothes they'd seen at the museum.

Ellie pulled her coat open a little, and saw a blue woollen dress, covered in the beautiful embroidery that Mum had loved so much. She'd said she wished she could do something like that…

Mum! Ellie plunged back towards the trees. Mum always seemed to wake up if she or Taylor got up in the night. She was probably searching for Ellie right now, and panicking. But where was the path?

Then the frightened cry came again, and

Essi blinked and shook her head. That was so strange... She'd been in a dream world – she'd almost felt like someone else. She was probably just getting too cold. She'd better hurry and warm herself up. She wasn't sure how late in the night it was – she didn't want to risk her family waking up and finding her gone.

Essi scanned the snowfield in front of her, trying to spot the injured creature. It would help if she knew what it was. It had better not be a wolf. Her heart thudded horribly. If it *was* a wolf, she was turning straight round again and running back to the cabin...

The cry sounded again, so much quieter now, as though the creature was losing hope, and Essi knew that even if it was a wolf, she couldn't leave it behind.

The snow flickered in front of her, and

Essi stopped abruptly. Was that something moving? A white hare, maybe, with its winter coat hiding it against the snow. She sighed. If the hare was caught in one of her father's snares, it probably wouldn't survive. And it would make a good meal for her family. The hunting had been unlucky the last few days and everyone was hungry. It would be best to put the poor thing out of its pain quickly.

She couldn't take it back to the cabin though, could she? How would she explain it? Perhaps the hare would be able to race away if she freed it. Essi crept closer – and then gasped as a pair of glittering amber eyes looked up into hers. Amber eyes lined with black, in a puff of white fur, almost whiter than the snow. A round button of a black nose. Black whiskers.

Not a hare – a fox.

THE ARCTIC FOX

Essi had seen them before, in the distance, often two foxes skittering and dancing after each other. She'd laughed at them playing.

She'd seen a few close up too – when her father carried them home after checking his traps and snares. They always seemed so much smaller then, hanging limply over his shoulder. It was as if they shrank when the spirit went out of them. She'd stroked the foxes' fur – thick, and soft, and warm! She could understand why the traders paid so well for it, even though she hated that her father had to trap them.

Essi knew it was strange to feel that way. Her father made offerings at the *seita* stone to please the spirits and thank them for sending him food for their family and furs to trade. If the fox was in the snare, then the spirits had meant for it to be caught. But it still felt wrong to make the wild, dancing foxes into something so quiet and small.

Cautiously, Essi approached the fox. Even though the little creature was trapped in one of Essi's father's snares, she wasn't helpless. The fox's teeth were needle sharp. She would probably be able to rip through Essi's mittens – and Essi was going to have to take those off, to loosen the snare.

"Shhh, shhh…" she murmured as she came closer, and the fox began to struggle violently. "Don't, you're just making it pull tighter! Oh, I wish you understood what I was trying to say. I only want to help…"

Back in the summer when everything hadn't frozen solid, her father had attached the snare to a sharpened stick, and hammered it deep into the ground. It was held fast in the stone-hard earth now – however much the fox fought, she wouldn't be able to pull it loose. The snare was made of reindeer sinew, strong and flexible. If the fox had known to drag it against a sharp stone she might have been able to wear it through, but her frantic pulling was just drawing the loop tighter around her neck.

At last the fox stopped struggling, sinking down into the snow instead, panting and coughing as the tight snare choked her. She glared at Essi, but Essi thought that the angry, frightened look in her eyes was lessening. As if she was giving in – and giving up. She was almost past caring what happened now.

"That's right," Essi whispered. "Just keep still for me." She crouched down, going to her knees and reaching carefully for the little fox. The fox snapped sharply once as Essi's hands came closer, but then she lay still, her breathing shallow.

Essi worked her fingers in between the snare and the thick white fur, trying to ease the loop wider so she could slip it back over the fox's head. The fox was quite still now, but Essi was sure she could feel her heart beating. Of course her heart would be pounding. She must be utterly terrified. Everything she knew of people – Sámi or the other fur trappers who came through their lands every so often – had taught her to be frightened of them.

"I'm sorry," Essi whispered. "It isn't fair.

You live here too. You were made to live here, weren't you? You even change your fur to fit with the seasons. Grey to match the rocks in the summer, and white to disappear into the snow in the winter. This is your place."

She sighed – and then suddenly the snare loosened, and she felt the loop pull open.

"At last!" She wriggled it further, until eventually the snare was wide enough to slip over the white fox's little, rounded ears.

Essi had expected the fox to shoot away at once, that she would hardly see her as her white coat blurred into the snow and the shimmering foxlight. But instead the little creature trembled, and staggered, as though it had been the snare itself that was holding her up. She slumped down on to Essi's reindeer-skin coat, her eyes closed.

Essi stared at her. Was she dead? Had she freed her too late? Or perhaps the shock of the trap had been too much for her. She had been fighting so hard. Very slowly, Essi stretched out her cold hand and laid it on the white fox's side, trying to feel her chest moving, her breath.

Nothing. No breath, no thumping heart. She was like one of the sad little white-furred things Essi's father brought home.

"No…" Essi whispered sadly. She ran her fingers through the thick fur, over and over.

And then the white fox coughed, and twitched, and her amber-gold eyes blinked open to gaze up at Essi.

Both of them froze. Essi stared down at the fox, wondering if she would bite. Should she shove the little creature away before she could snap? The fox's eyes slid frantically from side to side as she tried to work out her best escape route. She twitched again, as if trying to set off at a run – but her legs just weren't answering her. She had worn herself out fighting the snare and she didn't have the energy to flee. The fox stared back at Essi, clearly not understanding why she wasn't halfway across the snowfield by now. Then she sighed, laid her short, pointed muzzle down on her front paws, and closed her eyes.

Essi watched her, mouth a little open in surprise. Was the fox just going to sleep on her lap? It really looked like it. She wriggled her feet a little in her boots, trying to get more comfortable – they were going to sleep too. The cosy weight of the fox was welcome; Essi was getting cold from sitting still in the freezing night. She pulled her mittens back on, and then slipped her hands underneath the sleeping fox. The little creature only snuffled and slumped down even more, stretching herself across Essi's knees.

"I wonder what your name is," Essi whispered to her. "What did your mother and your brothers and sisters call you?" She smiled to herself. "Probably something that just sounded like Yip! or Grrr…" She eyed the perfect white fur, the thick cloud-like brush,

and smiled wider. "Åppås," she murmured.
That was the word for the best, most perfect
snow, fresh and clean without any tracks.
The little fox was Åppås – or she had been,
until Essi's family had caught her, and spoiled
her. It was up to Essi to make it right.

But how? She couldn't stop her father
hunting and trapping. He would snare more
foxes, Essi knew. It was no good promising the
fox that this would never happen again, even if
Essi wished she could. *Maybe one day…*

Food was the only thing Essi could think of
to give the fox – and it wasn't something she
and her family had much of. But she did have
a little piece of smoked reindeer meat in the
pocket of her coat. Her mother had given it to
her that morning, and she'd never got round
to eating it. Essi wriggled her hand out from

underneath the fox's fur and reached into her coat pocket, pulling out the dry strip ready for when Åppås woke up. As she looked back at the fox, she saw that her bright eyes were open and watching her hungrily.

"Oh! Did you smell it?" Essi whispered. "Here you are." She held out the meat, and the fox took it from her delicately, holding it between her teeth. She clambered stiffly to her feet and looked around, clearly checking for any danger. She glanced up at Essi again, her eyes brighter now, almost sparkling. Then she darted away, disappearing into the frozen snow in seconds. All Essi could see was the pinkish foxlight moving slowly across the frozen ground.

"Oh well…" Essi whispered, a little sadly. She felt as though she'd lost something special.

"Maybe I'll see you again. But it's probably better for you if I don't," she added seriously. "Stay away from us, little Åppås. Stay safe."

Ellie stared out across the snow, still watching for the little white fox. Eventually, she closed her eyes for a moment. Gazing at the the foxlight for so long had made them ache.

When she opened her eyes again, everything seemed different. Ellie couldn't work out what it was. She was out on the tundra, just above the patch of forest by her family's cabin. It wasn't far off morning, she thought, looking around anxiously. She ought to get back to the cabin soon, or her parents would wake up and see that she was missing. She didn't want them to be frightened, or Taylor.

She blinked.

Her brother was called Lemet.

No – Taylor, of course it was. She was dreaming again. That's what came of sitting about in the cold. What was she *doing* out here? Essi looked down at her hands, wondering what she'd done with her mittens. Her fingers felt so cold, they were stiff and aching. She was expecting to see reindeer-fur mittens. She knew she'd been wearing them, the mittens her mother had made for her.

But instead, she had warm waterproof gloves on, purple, with little sparkly snowflakes.

Ellie shook her head, trying to clear away the weird fogginess, the double memories. Was she Essi or Ellie? Where did she belong?

THE ARCTIC FOX

When was she? She stumbled to her feet
and staggered a little, trying to balance.
Her feet were almost numb and she could
barely feel them.

She'd got up in the middle of the night, called by the aurora – the foxlight. She'd wanted to go out and dance in it, to soak it up. That had definitely happened, for both of her selves. But which one *was* she? She began to stumble towards the trees, heading back to the cabin. Bewildering pictures of her family waiting for her flickered in her mind. Two different families. She was wearing Ellie's clothes, but Essi's memories were there too. Including the sad ones – the nights when she'd lain awake, hungry. Her strange mixed feelings about her father's animal trapping.

It was hard to hold all of that in her head at once. Ellie had been so angry about people trapping the foxes – but Essi understood, even if she didn't like it. Her family needed food. She knew what it was like to be hungry, really hungry, when Ellie didn't.

Essi also knew that very soon she was going to be too cold to carry on. A little feeling was coming into her feet now that she was moving, but she ached all over, and her fingers were still worryingly cold. She had to hurry and find her way back.

Except … she had some of Essi's memories, but not all of them. They were like photographs or films inside her head, and they were fading.

She couldn't remember the way home.

7

Ellie tucked her gloved hands under her arms, and stared around at the dark trees, their branches laden with snow. There were just – so many of them. She'd trekked across the snowy tundra for what felt like miles, looking for the howling fox. But she'd done it as Essi – Essi who knew how to follow trail signs and had lived in a cabin in the woods all her life. Essi knew where she was going. Ellie didn't.

"I have to walk," Ellie whispered to herself. Standing still was only making her feel colder. She set off towards the trees, trying not to think about how far the forest spread around the bare snowfield. It was only one very small cabin. How was she ever going to find it again?

"Stop it," she muttered to herself. "Don't give up before you've even started." It was something Dad said to her when she was being miserable about something. Usually learning her spelling words, but he'd said it when she was about to go away on Brownie holiday too, when she'd been worrying about being homesick. He'd been right – she'd loved it and had hardly missed home at all.

It was a little warmer once she was in among the trees, or at least less windy. Ellie could breathe in without the cold air hurting her chest. But it was frightening how many trees there seemed to be. They all looked the same too. Had she noticed any landmarks on the way?

Ellie tried to think. A tall, pointed rock, maybe? A tree with a fallen branch trailing down against the trunk? She couldn't see anything here but trees. And snow.

Ellie ploughed on, her feet moving more slowly with every step. The cold wasn't hurting as much now. It was making her sleepy. She couldn't feel her feet, but she didn't think it mattered any more. She'd find a place to sit down, somewhere safe and out of the cold, and have a rest. Then she'd be able to keep going and find the cabin. The problem was, nowhere was safe and out of the cold. Perhaps that didn't matter, Ellie decided. She only needed to have a bit of a rest. She sat down in the snow – just folding at the knees and slumping, really.

It was quite warm, she decided sleepily. Much warmer than it had been before, when she was holding the white fox. How strange. Ellie closed her eyes and curled herself tighter into a little ball.

She dreamed. The foxlight was swooping down around her now, wrapping her in gorgeous trailing sheets of colour. It was so soft, and it smelled nice, like hot chocolate, or her mum's flower perfume…

Something was nudging her. Ellie muttered
crossly and tried to push it away. It wasn't
time to get up yet. "Go away," she whispered.
Whoever it was didn't go away, though. They
nudged her again, a damp nose pressing
determinedly against her cheek. And then
they stood on her! Something was definitely
standing on top of her, and now a rough, raspy
tongue was licking her ear.

"It isn't time to get up!" Ellie said crossly, sitting up in the snow. "It's the middle of the night!"

The Arctic fox leaped off her shoulder and stood there looking at her doubtfully.

Ellie was so dazed with cold that for a moment the fox looked like a dark nose and a pair of dark-ringed amber eyes, just floating in the snow. Then she woke up a little more and saw her properly.

"Åppås! It's you!" Ellie looked around, and shook her head, trying to shake off the cold sleepiness. "You licked my ear…" she said. "You knew I shouldn't be sleeping in the snow… Have you been following me?"

Ellie staggered to her feet. "Thank you," she added, looking down at the white fox. "I might not have woken up if I'd stayed

there much longer. You're never supposed
to lie down in the snow, I know that! But it
looked so comfy, and it almost felt warm."
She shuddered. Then she looked hopefully
at Åppås. "I don't suppose you know the way
back to the cabin?"

It felt a bit strange asking her the way home,
but Ellie was pretty sure the fox had just
saved her life. "I suppose I saved you," she
murmured. "Or at least Essi did. And now
you're paying us back."

Ellie blinked. Was it some strange foxfire
magic that had called her out into the snow in
the middle of the night? Perhaps that first little
fox who swept the snow up into the sky had
made it all happen, to save one of her own.

Åppås set off, leading Ellie through the trees. Ellie wasn't sure how the little white fox knew the way – the woods weren't meant to be her territory after all. She seemed quite certain though, padding lightly over the snow, stopping here and there to sniff at a tree trunk or poke her nose into a pile of snow. Perhaps that first fox was still guiding them both. Ellie hoped so. It was almost silent in the woods, and darker than out on the tundra, since the thick trees stopped the foxfire light reaching the ground. Ellie wished she had a torch, but she had a feeling it would have scared Åppås away.

Then all at once, Åppås stopped, glancing around and scenting the air, nose lifted. This wasn't just finding the way, Ellie thought. The Arctic fox looked different – she looked worried, frightened even.

Ellie looked around too, wondering what the little fox could sense. Was it hunters? She wasn't completely sure which time they were in – she'd been trying not to think about it too much, because it was confusing, and scary – what if they were still in Essi's world, three hundred years or so before? Perhaps

Åppås could hear Essi's father, setting out
to trap more wild creatures. She shuddered.

"What is it?" she whispered to Åppås.

"Is someone coming?"

The white fox looked back at her uncertainly
for a moment, and then drew a few steps closer.

She was definitely frightened, Ellie thought.

The fox shook herself, the way Ellie did sometimes, trying to brush off her worries. Then she set off through the snow again, checking behind her to make sure Ellie was following. She stayed alert, though. Her ears were flickering, and every so often she would stop and freeze, and her ears would swivel.

There must be something behind them. Ellie couldn't hear it, or see it, but she was pretty sure Åppås could. The fox was far more used to this world than Ellie, even if she was a creature of the tundra. Perhaps it was just the eerie silence, but a strange dread began creeping up Ellie's spine, as she started to sense something following them. As though she could feel that they were being chased.

Hunted.

"Should we go faster?" she whispered to

Åppås, and in answer the white fox sped up, her paws padding quickly over the snow. Ellie stumbled and blundered behind her, trying to walk on feet that were still half numb and half aching. At least her hands were feeling a little better, they were tingly, but she could move her fingers easily now.

Ellie kept glancing behind them, trying to see what it was that had scared Åppås so much. Part of her didn't want to know... She couldn't see anything, anyway – just deeper shadows among the trees, and faint gleams of foxlight on the snow every so often. She couldn't help remembering that Mum had said there were wolves in the forests – but Mum had also promised that the wolves were shy, and scared of humans, and wouldn't want to come near...

Then, at last, she caught a faint glimpse of movement, worryingly close. She couldn't tell what it was, only that something had moved.

"Did you see that?" she hissed to Åppås, but the fox obviously had. She was closer to Ellie now, her teeth bared and the fur around her neck and shoulders fluffed up. She looked like she was getting ready to fight.

Whatever was lurking in the shadows seemed to realize it had been spotted. It slunk out from between two trees, eyeing Ellie and Åppås hungrily.

It was a cat – a huge cat. Not quite the size of a lion or a tiger, but still massive, and powerful.

They were called lynx, Ellie remembered. Mum had said maybe they might see one, and Ellie had been excited. But she'd been imagining seeing it from a snowmobile, with a guide to point it out, or maybe standing in the doorway of their cabin with a mug of hot chocolate while the lynx loped past, and Mum and Dad saying how lucky they'd been to catch sight of something so rare and special.

The lynx was spotted and striped in grey and black, a bit like an enormous tabby cat. It wasn't quite shaped like one though – its paws were massive, for walking on snow, and it only had a short tail. It had pointed ears too, with long black tufts sticking up, and thick fur around its neck – not quite a mane, more like a fluffy white beard.

THE ARCTIC FOX

In a zoo, Ellie would have thought it was gorgeous. Right now, it was terrifying.

The lynx was still padding towards them, and it seemed to be focusing on Åppås, Ellie thought – it had hardly looked at her. For a tiny, guilty second, Ellie was relieved, but then anger surged inside her. Essi in the past had tried so hard to rescue Åppås from the snare – and now Åppås was trying to help *her* get home. Ellie wasn't going to let anything happen to the white fox. She whipped round, looking frantically for something she could use to chase the huge cat away, but she wasn't quite sure what. Would it be scared of snowballs? There wasn't much else to hand. Except – there! Hanging down from one of the pine trees was a loose branch, still attached by the thinnest strip of bark.

THE ARCTIC FOX

Ellie ripped at it, hearing Åppås start to yip angrily behind her. At last she managed to yank the branch free, and she swung round, waving it wildly at Åppås and the lynx.

The white fox scuttled back towards her, and the lynx stared, almost comically shocked. It didn't seem to know what to do with itself. Eventually it growled at Ellie, and Ellie yelled back – a furious roar of her own – and swiped the branch at it. She wasn't close enough to actually hit it – did she even want to hit such a beautiful wild creature? – but she was close enough to be scary. The lynx tried to dodge around her, obviously still aiming for the smaller fox prey, but Åppås was carefully tucked up next to Ellie's legs. The lynx snorted, and Ellie wasn't sure if she was imagining the disgust in that snort.

It had had enough of this – a waste of time stalking through the trees, and now this strange creature shouting at it. It glared at them both and then slunk away, creeping back into the shadows among the trees.

Ellie and Åppås were alone again.

Åppås touched her nose gently against the side of Ellie's knee. Ellie couldn't feel the damp smudge, of course, not through her thick winter trousers, but she imagined that she could, and it was comforting. A grateful little touch. Then the white fox set off through the trees, leaving behind only a scuffed patch in the frozen snow to show where the fox and the lynx and the girl had had their stand-off.

Ellie kept hold of the branch, in case she needed it again.

They trudged on – Ellie was sure that Åppås

was tiring now too. The attack from the lynx must have terrified her as much as it had terrified Ellie. Their steps were shaky, and the little fox's head was down. It looked to Ellie as if she was plodding grimly through the snow, determined to see this duty done. Perhaps Åppås would be glad to see the back of her. But then Ellie remembered that gentle touch.

She sighed, and then her sigh turned into a noisy yawn that made Åppås look round in surprise. "Sorry!" Ellie murmured. "Oh…" She frowned at the trees ahead. Surely the spaces between them were larger now – and the night seemed lighter? There was more silvery moonlight filtering through. They were coming to the edge of the forest at last.

Ellie's heart beat faster, thumping with hope, and she glanced around eagerly. Where was the cabin? The white fox stared up at her patiently, and then almost pointed with her nose. She couldn't have been saying "Over there" any clearer if she'd spoken. And there it was. Nestled among the last of the trees, looking so home-like and cosy and wonderful that Ellie wanted to run to it and fling herself through the door, except she was just too tired.

"How did you know where to bring me?" Ellie asked, blinking away tears of relief. "Unless the fox who sweeps the snow into the sky told you, I suppose. Oh! Of course. You've been here before. Was it you chasing the squirrel? Did you see me watching you?"

Åppås ignored all of this and marched determinedly on towards the cabin. She wasn't leaving anything to chance, Ellie realized. She was making sure Ellie went right to the door. Together, they stumbled the last few steps, and Ellie collapsed on to the little wooden deck outside the cabin. It was sheltered by the overhanging roof and bare of snow.

"Thank you," she murmured to Åppås. "I wasn't sure I'd ever make it back here. I wouldn't have done if you hadn't shown me the way."

THE ARCTIC FOX

The little white fox hopped up on to the deck next to her and sat down, obviously glad of a chance to rest out of the icy wind too.

"This is the cabin *now*," Ellie said slowly, looking behind her at the pretty red-and-white candle decorations in the window. "I'm pretty sure it is, anyway." She swallowed hard. "I was scared it would be Essi's cabin. That it would be her family asleep in there, not mine." She eyed Åppås uncertainly. "I'm not sure when you are. Or were… But I'm so glad you're OK. You will be careful, won't you? You've got to go back, and there's still that lynx in the woods."

Åppås yawned, as if to say that she wasn't afraid of any lynx. Then she stood up, stretched out her front paws, and leaned over to nudge Ellie again – this time, she brushed her cold black nose gently against Ellie's cheek, like a kiss. She looked at Ellie for a moment, amber-gold eyes catching the last gleam of the foxlight sky, and then she jumped down from the deck and pattered away into the trees.

Ellie gazed after her, watching as the huge snow-soft brush of a tail disappeared into the shadows, and then stood up. She turned, raised the door latch as quietly as she could, and slipped inside the cabin.

"Ellie. Ellie."

Ellie's hands clenched tightly around the corner of the duvet. Where was she? *When* was she? Was that Taylor waking her up, or was it some unknown brother or sister from hundreds of years before?

"Ell-*eeee*…"

It was definitely Taylor. Only Taylor said her name like that. Ellie opened her eyes and smiled at him sleepily.

"What is it?" she asked, glancing around the room – yes, there was her bag, and the clothes she'd been wearing yesterday on the chair. She was back in her own time again. It was lighter, but still not very light – it was hard to tell the time when the whole day was a dim twilight, but Ellie thought it was still very early.

"Where did you go?"

Ellie looked sharply back at Taylor. "What do you mean?"

"When I woke up in the middle of the night you weren't here."

Ellie was about to deny it, but Taylor sounded really worried and she didn't like the idea of lying about Åppås and Essi and the snow fox. Their night together had been too special – even if it had been frightening as well.

"I had to go and help someone," she said cautiously. She didn't want Taylor dashing off to tell Mum and Dad that she'd been wandering around in the middle of the night.

Taylor climbed up on to Ellie's bed and wriggled under the covers next to her. "Tell me," he said, leaning against her shoulder. He was very warm, and very real, and Ellie slipped her arm around him. "Well… I woke up in the middle of the night, and I could see the foxfire light, shining across the floor…"

Ellie and Taylor were both still asleep, curled together in Ellie's bed, when their mum came to wake them later in the morning.

"Oh, Taylor, did you have a bad dream?" she asked worriedly, and Ellie blinked. She hadn't thought to ask Taylor not to tell Mum and Dad about her adventure. But Taylor only smiled at Mum.

"I woke up, and Ellie told me a story."

Ellie let out a quiet, relieved breath.

"That was kind, Ellie, thank you! Do you want to get up now, you two? Dad's made breakfast, it's nearly ready. And then we're going on a husky sleigh ride later on!"

THE ARCTIC FOX

The huskies were beautiful, and friendly, even though they kept on barking. Ellie couldn't help thinking how fox-like they looked with their sharp noses and pointed ears. She kept seeing Åppås everywhere, and then of course it was just a white husky, or even a pile of snow.

THE ARCTIC FOX

It would be better if Ellie didn't see her again, of course. The forest around the cabin wasn't the right place for an Arctic fox – she should be out on the tundra, far away from people. But it was hard not to keep looking.

The husky sleighs went much faster than the reindeer had. They whooshed along snowy forest paths and Ellie came back breathless and excited. It was an amazing last day of the holiday. The best thing was that they were going home just in time for Christmas, so there was none of that end-of-holiday sadness, even when they were packing.

Still, it was hard to shut the door of the little cabin and look out into the woods one last time. Ellie stood by the hire car, gazing into the trees. That was just a snowdrift. There weren't any sparkling amber eyes staring back at her?

"Time to go, Ellie." Mum shut the boot and came to give her a hug. "It's been wonderful, hasn't it?"

Ellie turned away from the empty forest to hug her back. "The best," she whispered. "Thank you. I'll never forget it."

Ellie sat up in bed, sleepy, but sure that something exciting was about to happen. She had a *good* feeling, and she couldn't remember why. Then it came back to her, all of a sudden. It was Christmas morning!

She leaned over to look at her clock. Just before seven, and Mum and Dad had said absolutely no waking them up before six and that she wasn't to wake up Taylor. There was no harm in seeing if he was almost awake, though… Ellie bounced out of bed, admiring the lumpy stocking looped around her bedpost. Surely Taylor would be awake any minute? She crept along the landing and peered in through his open door. Her little brother was sitting up in bed, his face already smeared with chocolate.

"You're not meant to open things yet!" Ellie told him. "Let's go and wake them up."

Ellie had been planning to tiptoe in and wake Mum and Dad up gently, but Taylor yelled, "It's Christmas!" and bounced out of bed, racing along to Mum and Dad's room. Dad groaned as Taylor leaped on top of him, and Mum sat up.

"You lasted longer than I thought you would. Why don't you both bring your stockings in here? I'm just going to make a very quick cup of tea for me and Dad."

Ellie curled up on the end of their bed, poking curiously at her Christmas stocking and wondering what the different parcels were. There was a book in there, definitely. And she could see a candy cane sticking out. She just about managed to resist tearing into the wrapping paper until Mum came back with the tea. Dad took a big gulp and sighed. "OK. I'm ready now. Let's see what Santa brought."

Ellie had been right about the book, but her stocking was packed with other things too. A Lego reindeer, which was a brilliant reminder of their holiday, some chocolate, a huge lollipop. Socks, which was quite funny inside a stocking, and some beautiful glittery pens and a notebook.

Once she'd unwrapped everything and she

was leaning against Mum's shoulder, nibbling at a little bit of her candy cane and looking at the book, Dad leaned over to his bedside table and handed Ellie a little parcel wrapped up in snowflake paper, with a twirly silver ribbon.

"This one's from me and Mum," he told Ellie. "It's a bit little to put under the tree – we were worried it would get lost."

"Thank you!" Ellie took the parcel and eyed it curiously, wondering what it could be. She looked up at Mum and Dad and found them exchanging a glance, as if they were really excited about this present too. It was something special, Ellie was sure. She slipped off the ribbon and started to undo the tape, peeling it back carefully.

Inside was a little velvet box – a jewellery

box! Ellie didn't have much jewellery, just a few bracelets that she'd made from bead kits, and the box looked very grown-up. Her fingers were trembling a little as she tried to open the catch.

Inside the box, on a soft silky lining, was a necklace. A pendant that flashed foxfire in Ellie's shaking fingers. It was a little silver fox's head, with a piece of glowing spectrolite set into it, between the fox's ears. Ellie turned it slowly this way and that, watching the Northern Lights glimmer and swirl.

"Do you like it?" Dad asked hopefully.

"It's beautiful," Ellie whispered. "So perfect." Then she looked up at them. "Why did you choose a fox?" How could they have known?

"Oh, well, you loved those Arctic fox photos," Mum said thoughtfully. "I know we didn't actually see any Arctic foxes, but there was that beautiful story we heard about the Northern Lights and a fox. It just seemed right." She leaned over. "Do you want me to help you put it on, Ellie?"

Ellie turned to let Mum fasten the necklace around her neck, and then she lifted up the pendant to look at the little fox face. Was she imagining that it looked like Åppås? She stroked the smooth stone, feeling the same wild winter magic she'd felt as Essi on that strange night. She was dancing in the snow again, surrounded by the foxfire light. And she knew that somewhere there was a little white fox, watching from between the trees.

Turn the page for an extract from

One rare owl. One magical discovery.

SKY

From MULTI-MILLION bestselling author

Holly Webb

Lara peered out of the train window, watching the dark wild hills pass by. The journey had been exciting to start with, but now she was sick of being cooped up and starting to feel a bit grumpy. She hadn't slept well either – the top bunk in the sleeper compartment had been nearly as big as her bed at home, but the train rattled and bumped and shook, and she'd kept waking up. Lara was sure her mum had struggled to sleep too. She looked even paler than usual, and there were huge purply shadows under her eyes.

"Are you OK?" Lara asked, turning back from the window, her voice gruff. She hated asking – what would she do if Mum said no? Lara's mum had been ill for a while, nearly a whole year, but she was getting a lot better. Sometimes Lara found it hard to believe that she was really recovering.

Mum smiled at her, and then at Dad, who whipped round to stare at her, his face frightened. "I'm fine! Honestly." She patted Dad's hand, and then reached over the table to hold Lara's hand too. "The train was a bit noisy, wasn't it? But I still think it was a good idea of yours to take the sleeper, Steve. It's lovely to get the journey done overnight, and not to have to sit in the car for hours and hours. We'll be at the station in about forty-five minutes, I think. Enough time for you to finish off that breakfast, Lara."

Lara nodded, picking at her croissant. She was looking forward to seeing Gran and Grandad – it was ages since they'd last visited, and video calls just weren't the same as the real thing. You couldn't hug through a screen. Her grandparents lived in a cottage in the Highlands of Scotland, almost as far away as you could get and still be in Britain. It was at least a ten-hour journey in the car, and usually Mum and Dad and Lara drove there in the summer holidays. Mum hadn't been up to it this summer, so they hadn't been to visit for a year and a half. It seemed like forever.

"I'll go and make sure everything's packed away in our sleeping cabins," Dad said. "Back in a minute."

"I'm so excited we're having Christmas at Fir Cottage," Mum told Lara, as Dad headed off between the seats. "I loved Christmas there when I was growing up – with that huge fireplace to sit around, it's a house that's perfect for winter. It's magical. Your gran told me they've had a bit of snow already, and there's more forecast!"

Lara brightened up. A proper snowy Christmas would be brilliant, and she'd never been to Scotland in the winter before. There was even a ski resort not far from her grandparents' cottage. Except … the best bit about snow was getting to meet up with friends and have snowball fights, or make snow angels. She and her friend Anisha had made amazing balls of coloured ice when it was really cold last winter – they'd filled balloons with water and food colouring, and left pink ice bubbles all over Anisha's front garden.

Anisha hadn't said much when Lara explained she was going to be away for most of the Christmas holidays, but she'd looked so disappointed. Lara hadn't had much time to spend with her friends over the last few months – it had been so tricky, fitting in everything round Mum's hospital appointments. Lara felt like she'd spent days in waiting rooms. And when they had been at home, Mum had been too tired to have people round. Now she was getting better, Lara had been hoping for a Christmassy sleepover…

Still … Lara wanted so much for her mum to be happy. Happy and well. She could do stuff with Anisha when they got back home, there would be a couple of days before school started again.

"Is that snow up there on those hills?" she asked, pressing her nose against the train window.

"Yes, oh, look!" Mum's voice was high and squeaky with delight. "Oh, Lara, I'm so glad we're here, it's a real treat for me. And there are so many lovely things we can do. We can visit the reindeer again, do you remember doing that last time we were here? It'll be even better in the snow! And Dad says he'll take you to the ski slopes."

Lara looked back at Mum, and saw how her eyes were sparkling. Suddenly, she didn't mind being away from home at Christmas at all.

As they stepped down from the train with all the cases, Gran came hurrying across the platform to seize Mum in a hug, and Grandad scooped Lara up and swung her around. Lara couldn't stop laughing, swept away with all the happiness and excitement.

"Oh, we've got so much to tell you," Gran said, as they began to pick everything up and head through the station to the car. "All the lovely things we've got planned. And you'll never guess what your grandad saw yesterday, Lara. Something so special."

For a tiny moment, Lara wondered if Gran meant something magical – little elves, perhaps, peering in between the trees that surrounded the cottage, or a snow spirit, dancing down out of the sky. Then she smiled at herself for being silly. It was Mum talking about how special the cottage was that had done it. And the sight of snow! Now they were stepping out of the station doors, she could see the sky properly – grey and heavy and snow-laden, with a few tiny, lazy snowflakes fluttering down.

"Oh, it's snowing!" she cried, gazing up at the thick clouds.

"Yes, and there's going to be a whole lot more of it, I promise you that," Grandad said, as he pulled out the car keys. "But you still haven't guessed, Lara. What do you think I saw?"

"A pine marten?" Lara asked hopefully. Grandad had emailed her a video of a pine marten on their garden bird table a few weeks before, a gorgeous dark-furred little creature, and she really wanted to see one for herself.

"Oh…" Grandad waved the keys around as though pine martens were nothing. "He's back every other day, Lara, he'd probably steal your breakfast toast out of your hand if you let him. No, something much more exciting than that."

"I give up," Lara said, smiling at him. She could see he was desperate to tell her.

Grandad drew himself up very straight and said, in a deep, impressive voice. "A ... snowy ... owl!"

"Oh…" Lara nodded politely. She wasn't really as interested in birds as she was in other animals. And she couldn't help feeling that owls were a bit spooky.

"They're incredibly rare!" Grandad told her, looking slightly disappointed. "You only see them – oh, once every few years. They usually live in the Arctic, you see."

"What, like polar bears?" Lara asked, surprised. That was a bit more special.

"Exactly! They used to nest in Scotland sometimes, but there hasn't been a breeding pair here for nearly fifty years, and that was on Fetlar, one of the Shetland Isles. They're very occasional winter visitors here in the Cairngorms these days. I've only ever seen one once before, and that was years ago."

"Ian, we need to get in the car," Gran said, in a very patient voice. "It's cold. And Marie needs to stay warm, remember."

"Oh! Yes." Grandad unlocked the car. "I'll tell you more about snowy owls once we're home, Lara. You'll be very excited."

Dad grinned at Lara and nudged her with his elbow. "I don't think you've got any choice."

Back at the cottage, Gran led Lara up to a tiny little room right up under the roof, the one she always slept in. There was a steep, narrow staircase just for her, and it opened straight out into the bedroom. The ceiling sloped right down to the floor and there was a tiny window that looked out on to the garden – which was already flecked with patches of snow.

"Unpack your things in here," Gran said, showing Lara a chest of drawers. "And then come and have some hot chocolate. I got some of those little marshmallows you like. And that squirty cream."

Lara hurriedly shoved her clothes into the drawers, pulled on her fleecy slippers, and raced back down the staircase.

HOLLY WEBB

Holly Webb started out as a children's book editor and wrote her first series for the publisher she worked for. She has been writing ever since, with over one hundred and fifty books to her name. Holly lives in Berkshire, with her husband and three children. Holly's pet cats are always nosying around when she is trying to type on her laptop.

For more information about Holly Webb visit:

www.holly-webb.com